To Honey—such a sweetie and

a friend for only a short time

GROSSET & DUNLAP
Published by the Penguin Group
Penguin Group (USA) LLC, 375 Hudson Street, New York, New York 10014, USA

USA | Canada | UK | Ireland | Australia | New Zealand | India | South Africa | China

penguin.com
A Penguin Random House Company

Text copyright © 2009, 2014 Sue Bentley. Illustrations copyright © 2009 Angela Swan. Cover illustration copyright © 2009 Andrew Farley. First printed in Great Britain in 2009 by Penguin Books Ltd. First published in the United States in 2014 by Grosset & Dunlap, a division of Penguin Young Readers Group, 345 Hudson Street, New York, New York 10014. GROSSET & DUNLAP is a trademark of Penguin Group (USA) LLC. Printed in the USA.

Library of Congress Cataloging-in-Publication Data is available.

ISBN 978-0-448-46798-6   10 9 8 7 6 5 4 3

Sparkling Skates

SUE BENTLEY

Illustrated by Angela Swan

Grosset & Dunlap
An Imprint of Penguin Group (USA) LLC

Prologue

The young silver-gray wolf sped across the ice. Dark clouds were gathering overhead, and it began to snow. Storm lifted his head. A big snowflake landed on the young wolf's nose, and he licked it off. It felt good to be back in his homeland.

Suddenly a fierce howl split the still air.

"Shadow!" Storm gasped. The

powerful lone wolf who had attacked the Moon-claw pack and wounded Storm's mother was very close.

There was a flash of bright golden light and a shower of dazzling sparks. Where the young wolf had been standing there now crouched a tiny puppy with fluffy black fur, a stocky body, and short little legs.

Storm scampered forward, his little puppy heart beating fast. He hoped this disguise would protect him from his enemy.

The snow was falling thickly now. It swirled around Storm as he tore toward a thick clump of pine trees. He needed to find somewhere to hide, and quickly. His breath fogged in the cold air as he scrambled into the trees.

A large dark shape moved between the

trunks, and Storm saw wolf eyes gleaming through the curtain of snow. He caught his breath and skidded to a halt, ready to turn and run away as fast as he could.

"Storm! This way, quickly!" the wolf called in a soft growl.

"Mother." Storm sighed with relief. He rushed forward and weaved through the trees until he reached the she-wolf.

"It is good to see you again, my son," Canista rumbled, licking her disguised cub's fluffy black fur and small square muzzle.

Storm yipped a greeting. He wriggled his stocky little body and wagged his stumpy tail as he licked his mother's face. "I have come back to lead the Moon-claw pack!"

Canista showed her sharp teeth in a

proud smile. "Bravely said, but now is not the time. Shadow still wants to be leader, and he is too strong for you. I remain weak from his poisoned bite."

Storm's midnight-blue eyes narrowed with anger and sorrow. He knew that his mother was right, but he was reluctant to leave her.

"The other wolves will not follow Shadow—they are waiting for you. Go back to the other world. Return when you are stronger and your magic is more powerful." As Canista finished speaking, her eyes clouded with pain.

Storm leaned close and huffed out a warm puppy breath, which glinted with thousands of tiny gold sparkles. The mist swirled around Canista's injured paw and then disappeared into her gray fur.

Canista gave a sigh of relief as a tiny bit of her strength returned. But before Storm could complete the healing, another terrifying howl rang out, sounding much closer. Heavy paws thundered against the ground as a huge wolf crashed through the trees, and Storm could hear harsh breathing.

"Shadow knows you are here! Go now, Storm! Save yourself," Canista urged.

Storm whimpered as dazzling gold sparks bloomed in his fluffy black fur and he felt the power surging through him. The gold glow around him grew brighter. And brighter . . .

Chapter
ONE

"I can't wait to ask Mom and Dad about having figure-skating lessons!" Lauren Medley said as she and Jemila came out of the White Water ice rink.

"It would be great if you joined the Ice Academy with me!" Jemila said, her dark eyes sparkling. "We can go to classes together. Maggie, our coach, is great."

Lauren smiled at her best friend. Jemila

was in the same class at school and was an amazing figure skater. She was going to be performing in the show at the rink in a few weeks' time.

"Ice skating's so different from everything else I've ever tried. I love it so much, and I know it's something I really want to do," Lauren enthused.

Jemila smiled. "I think Maggie noticed that. She told me that she'd like to meet you sometime."

"Really? That's fantastic. Here's Mom now. Fingers crossed!" Lauren flicked back her shoulder-length fair hair as she ran over to her mom's car and opened the door. "Hi, Mom. Is it okay if we give Jemila a ride home?"

Lauren's mom nodded. "Yes, of course it is. Hop in, you two."

"Thanks, Mrs. Medley," Jemila said politely as she climbed into the backseat.

"Did you have a nice time at the rink?" Lauren's mom asked her as she began to drive.

"The best! I've been practicing some new moves. I'm getting really good at skating," Lauren replied. "And guess what?

Jemila's going to do a solo performance at the figure-skating show!"

"Congratulations!" Mrs. Medley smiled at Jemila in the rearview mirror. "We'll have to get tickets to come and watch you."

"I really love ice skating, and I want to be a figure skater, too, Mom," Lauren said eagerly. "So can I join the Ice Academy with Jemila? Some other girls from my class at school are going to join, too. And we're all—" She stopped as she saw that her mom was glancing across at her with raised eyebrows.

"So—figure skating's your latest craze, is it? What happened to BMX biking? You were nuts about that a few months ago," Mrs. Medley commented.

"I know, but this is different. I was terrible at that other stuff, but I'm good at figure skating! Even Maggie, the coach,

thinks I show promise. Isn't that great?"
Lauren said eagerly.

"Hmmm." Her mom rolled her eyes.
She turned on to a treelined road and drew
up outside a redbrick house.

"Thanks for the ride. See you at school
tomorrow, Lauren!" Jemila called as she got
out and walked toward her house.

"Bye!" Lauren waved.

As they drove off, Lauren chewed her
nails nervously. "So, when can I start figure-
skating classes?" she finally said.

"I'm not sure how I feel about this
idea," her mom said. "Let's wait until we
get home before we discuss it. I want to see
what your dad has to say."

"Okay." Lauren just about managed
not to say anything more. She was feeling
hopeful as she followed her mom into their

house. Her dad was really easygoing. He was bound to let her take ice-skating lessons.

But she was disappointed this time. "I'm sorry, but I agree with your mom," Mr. Medley decided after Lauren and her mom had finished talking. "We've already paid for tennis lessons *and* bought you a BMX bike. It doesn't make sense to shell out for skates and figure-skating lessons when you'll probably lose interest in about five minutes."

"But I won't! Not this time—honest!" Lauren promised. She knew that she really meant it this time. "And you won't even have to buy me skates. Jemila's promised to give me her old ones!"

"It sounds like you and Jemila have

got this all worked out," her dad said,
raising his eyebrows.

"We have!" she said hopefully, giving
him her best pleading smile.

Her dad shook his head slowly. "Even so,
I'm sorry, Lauren, but the answer's the same."

Lauren knew when she was beaten. She
sighed as she trudged out of the room and
went upstairs.

"Great! Everyone in my class is joining
up. Except me," she murmured glumly,
her spirits sinking. She imagined all the

lonely evenings while her friends had fun without her. What she wanted most of all was to pursue her dream of figure skating.

Just as Lauren reached the top step, there was a dazzling flash of bright gold light and a silent explosion of sparks that lit up the entire hallway.

"Oh!" Lauren gasped, rubbing her eyes. When she could see again, she noticed that a tiny fluffy puppy with black fur and a little square muzzle stood there.

"Can you help me, please?" it woofed.

Chapter
TWO

Lauren's jaw dropped and she gaped at the tiny puppy in complete astonishment. Was she imagining things?

She rubbed her eyes and looked again, but the puppy still stood there. It was gazing up at her with the biggest, brightest midnight-blue eyes she had ever seen.

"Where . . . where did you come from? How did you get in here?" Lauren asked, puzzled.

"I used my magic to come here from far away. My name is Storm, of the Moon-claw pack. What is yours?" the puppy yapped softly.

Lauren did a double take. "Whoa! You really *can* talk! I thought I'd imagined that, too!" She swallowed. "I'm Lauren. Lauren Medley. I live here with my mom and dad."

Storm bowed his little head. "I am

honored to meet you, Lauren."

"Um . . . me too," Lauren said, still having trouble taking this all in. As she bent down to make herself seem less big and frightening to this amazing puppy, she remembered something he had said. "Why do you need my help?"

Storm laid back his ears, and his little muzzle wrinkled nervously. "An evil lone wolf called Shadow is looking for me. He attacked our Moon-claw pack and killed my father and brothers, and wounded my mother, so that he might lead the wolves. But it is *my* destiny."

Lauren frowned. "How can you lead a wolf pack? You're just a tiny pu—"

"Stand back, please," Storm ordered. As Lauren stood up and backed slowly into her bedroom, there was another dazzling flash of golden light and the tiny black puppy disappeared. In its place, almost filling the entire hallway, stood an impressive young wolf with silver-gray fur and a thick neck ruff that twinkled with thousands of lights, like glittering yellow fireflies.

"Storm?" Lauren eyed the powerful wolf's big teeth nervously.

"Yes, it is me. Do not be afraid," Storm rumbled in a soft velvety growl.

Before Lauren had time to get used to seeing Storm as his true self, there was a final, even brighter flash of light, and a fountain of sparks sprinkled down all around Lauren, crackling harmlessly to the carpet.

When Lauren's sight cleared, she saw that Storm was a tiny, cute, helpless puppy once more. "Wow! That's a great disguise," she breathed. "No one would know that you're not really a cute little Scottie dog."

"Shadow will know it is me, if he finds me. I need to hide now," Storm whined.

Lauren saw that the tiny puppy was beginning to tremble all over. She felt a surge of protectiveness and gently picked him up. Storm snuggled into her arms as she stroked his fluffy black fur.

"You can live here with me in my bedro—" Lauren paused as she realized

that there was no way her mom and
dad were going to let her have a puppy.
They'd just think it was another one of her
impulsive, half-baked ideas, especially after
the figure-skating discussion. "Oh, I don't
think you can stay here after all," she said
sadly.

Storm nodded. "I understand. Thank you
for your kindness. I will find someone else to
help me."

But Lauren wasn't ready to lose her
magical new friend so quickly. She thought
hard. "Maybe I can hide you in my bedroom.
I could make you a bed inside my closet, but
you'd need to stay really quiet and not run
around or anything when Mom and Dad are
in the house. It might be really boring for
you, though."

Storm tipped up his intelligent little

face and blinked at her. "I would like to stay here in your room. It is a safe place. And I will use my magic, so that only you will be able to see and hear me."

"You can make yourself invisible? Cool! There's no problem then!" Lauren said eagerly.

She opened her closet and began throwing out old pairs of sneakers and a box of old dolls and teddy bears to make room for a bed for Storm.

"Lauren? I hope you're not too upset about . . . Hello, what are you up to?" asked a surprised voice from the open door.

Lauren whipped around to see her mom standing there. In all the excitement of finding Storm, she hadn't heard anyone coming up the stairs. "I thought I'd . . .

um . . . clean out . . . um, some old
clothes and toys and . . . um, stuff," she
said hastily.

Mrs. Medley took a step forward. She
put the back of her hand to her forehead
and pretended to feel faint. "You're
cleaning your room without being asked
to? Wonders will never cease, Lauren
Medley!"

Lauren flashed an anxious grin.

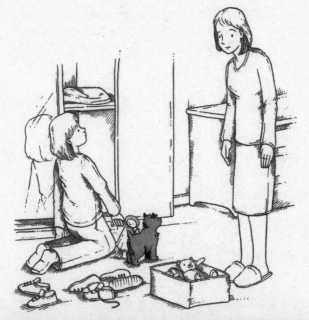

She tensed as her mom seemed to look straight at the tiny black puppy who sat on the floor beside her. But when her mom took no notice of Storm, Lauren felt herself relax, as she realized that he must have already made himself invisible.

A secret smile crossed Lauren's face. Perhaps she wouldn't be all by herself while everyone else was ice skating at the academy, after all.

Chapter
THREE

Lauren woke early on Monday morning. She'd been having a wonderful dream about gliding gracefully over the ice in pretty white skates and a shimmering costume trimmed with sparkling white feathers.

The feathers were tickling her nose. Lauren lifted a hand to brush them away, and then she realized that she had her cheek

pressed against Storm's soft, fluffy black fur.

She grinned with delight as she gathered the tiny puppy close for a cuddle. "Hello, you," she crooned. "Did you sleep well?"

"Yes, thank you. I feel safe here," Storm woofed, lifting his head to lick her chin with his little pink tongue.

"I'm glad," Lauren said. "Because I love having you living with me." She told him all about her dream. "I was playing

Sleeping Beauty in a fabulous ice show. Being a top figure skater was so amazing!"

Storm put his head to one side, his dewy eyes bright. "What is figure skating? Winter is very cold in my homeland, and lakes become covered with ice. But we do not skate on them."

"It's something people do for fun. We wear special shoes with metal blades to skate across the ice. But you have to practice a lot and learn to do jumps and twists and stuff in time to music to be a figure skater," Lauren explained.

Storm nodded. "It sounds very exciting. Are you going to do this?"

"I want to, more than anything. But I don't think it's going to happen," Lauren said, her whole body drooping back against the comforter.

"Why is that?" Storm's furry little face creased in concern.

"Mom and Dad think that I'll get bored with figure skating, so they won't pay for me to join the Ice Academy, and be coached, like all my friends. I did used to get bored with things easily when I was younger," Lauren explained honestly, "but I've changed. I know I have. It means everything to me to become a figure skater. If I could just find some way to prove it, Mom and Dad might change their minds and let me join."

"Is joining the Ice Academy the only way to get better at figure skating?" Storm yapped.

"It really is—unless I had my own private ice rink. Then I could practice whenever I wanted to!" Lauren joked glumly. "But that's never going to happen. So I might as well *totally* give up on the idea. Anyway, this is my problem. Don't you worry about me, Storm."

Lauren forced herself to cheer up as she threw back the covers and jumped out of bed. She was usually a happy person and, after all, she had Storm to keep her company now. "Time to get up. I've got to get ready for school."

Storm watched as Lauren began pulling on her school uniform, a thoughtful expression on his little square face.

Lauren smuggled some food upstairs for Storm after she finished her breakfast. She stood by, watching him slurping up the cereal and milk. "Sorry, but that's all there is for now. I'll get you some real dog food on my way home from school."

Storm was licking milk from his chops. "That was very nice. Thank you."

Lauren beamed at him. He looked so cute with a white milk mustache on his little black muzzle. It was hard to believe that the tiny helpless puppy was really an impressive young wolf.

"Will you be okay hiding up here while I'm at school?" she asked.

"I will come with you!" Storm yapped, his midnight-blue eyes gleaming.

Lauren wasn't sure if it was a good idea to have a lively puppy bounding around the classroom—even if he was invisible. But Storm looked so eager to come with her that she smiled and gave in. "Well . . . all right, then."

"Are you ready, Lauren? I'll be in the car," her mom called up the stairs.

"Okay. I'm coming!" Lauren answered. She turned back to Storm. "Mom's dropping me off on her way to work. Why don't you get in my book bag for now?"

Storm nodded. Lauren opened her bag, and he immediately jumped in and curled up next to her purple fake-fur pencil case.

Ten minutes later, Lauren stood at the school gates and waved good-bye as her mom drove away. "Here's Jemila. She's my best friend," she whispered to Storm as four girls came walking down the street toward her and Storm. "Becky, Katie, and Padmini are all my classmates, too."

"Hi, Lauren. Here are those skates I promised you," Jemila said as she reached

her friend. She handed her a drawstring
bag.

Lauren smiled gratefully as she took
the bag. "Thanks. But I don't think I'll be
needing them now. Mom and Dad won't
let me join the Ice Academy. They think I
won't keep it up. I've tried to tell them I
will, but they won't listen."

"Oh. That's awful," Jemila said. "Why don't you keep the skates anyway, in case they change their minds?"

"And pigs might fly!" Lauren said glumly.

"Tough luck," said Becky, wrinkling her nose sympathetically.

"Thanks," Lauren said. Becky was slim with a heart-shaped face and light-brown hair, and she was very popular in class. Her parents always bought her the latest things, and she always looked amazing. But no one minded, because she wasn't snooty to anyone and was very generous.

"Look! Dad got me the latest copy of *Silver Blades*," Becky said, taking a glossy magazine out of her bag. "There are some really cool figure-skating costumes. I'm going to get him to buy me one."

"Let's see!" Katie and Padmini chorused. The three of them crowded around the magazine, chattering excitedly about leotards and the latest designer skates. Lauren gazed longingly at the other girls as they wandered away into the playground.

Jemila hesitated and Lauren could tell that her best friend wanted to join the other girls. She wouldn't have blamed her

if she did, but Jemila linked arms with
Lauren instead.

Lauren beamed at her friend, pleased
that Jemila had chosen to walk to class
with her. But she couldn't help thinking
sadly about how all four of the other
girls would be meeting up each night for
lessons at the ice rink, while Lauren stayed
at home watching boring TV.

Lauren slipped her hand inside her
book bag. Storm woofed softly and
immediately began licking her fingers.
Lauren began to feel a little bit better, glad
that she would have her secret fluffy friend
to keep her company.

Chapter
FOUR

Lauren groaned as she sat looking down at her math workbook. She didn't seem able to concentrate today, and it was taking her forever to work through the problems. All she could think about was ice skating.

She sat back in her chair. Luckily it wouldn't be long until the bell rang for the end of class. Craning her neck,

Lauren looked around the room, but there
was no sign of Storm.

She wondered what he was up
to. Storm had finished exploring the
classroom an hour ago and had slipped out
to search for other interesting smells to
snuffle up.

Just then, Lauren saw a tiny black
form squeeze back inside the half-open
classroom door. She smiled to herself as
the mischievous magical pup scampered
toward her between the rows of desks. She
was still getting used to the idea that only
she could see him and hear him talking.

As soon as Storm reached Lauren,
he leaped straight up into the air, trailing
invisible sparks behind him like a rocket
taking off. He landed—*plonk!*—right on
her math book.

"Storm! I hope you haven't
got dirty paws! My teacher will go
bananas if I mess up my book!" Lauren
whispered, grinning, as she gently lifted
him aside.

Storm frowned. He lifted all four
paws in turn and examined them,
and then nodded, satisfied. "They are
all clean!" he yapped, sitting down
beside her. His stumpy little tail began
thumping loudly against the desk.

Lauren smothered a giggle and

quickly reached out to put her hand over his tail to muffle the sound. But she wasn't quick enough. Becky, who sat directly in front

of her, glanced around. She looked puzzled.

"What?" Lauren said innocently.

"I could have sworn I just heard a drumbeat or something," Becky said. When Lauren looked blank, she shrugged. "Weird. I must have imagined it." She turned around again and went back to her work.

Lauren smiled to herself, imagining the look on Becky's face if she found out an amazing magic puppy was sitting on Lauren's desk!

Quickly checking that no one else was looking her way, she whispered to Storm,

"Did you have a good time finding things to explore?"

Storm nodded, his midnight-blue eyes widening. "I have just been into a big room with shelves full of lots and lots of books."

"That's the school library," Lauren said, wondering why Storm had chosen to spend time in there. "Didn't you find it a bit boring?"

Storm shook his head, looking very pleased with himself. "No, it was very interesting!"

Lauren was about to ask him exactly what he had been doing in the library when the bell rang.

"All right, class. Put your work away," the teacher ordered.

There was a sudden noise of chairs

scraping as everyone began getting up to
go home. Lauren stuffed her schoolbooks
into her bag and then made space for
Storm to jump inside as well. Picking
up the other bag, which held the skates,
Lauren went outside with Jemila.

As the two of them walked to the
school gates, Lauren saw that her mom was
parked across the street. "Do you want a
ride home, Jemila?" she offered.

"Thanks, but Becky already asked if I'd
walk home with her. You don't mind, do
you?" Jemila asked.

"No, of course not," Lauren said,
although she did a bit.

"Okay, I'll see you in the morning
then." Jemila jogged toward Becky, who
was waiting a short distance away. Padmini
and Katie hurried forward to join them,

and the four girls walked off together.

Storm was sitting up with his front paws looped over the side of her bag. "Is something wrong?" he barked as Lauren stared wistfully after her friends.

"I'm just feeling a bit left out," Lauren admitted in a whisper. "All my friends are excited about figure skating. It's all they talk about. But there's no point in joining in, is there?"

Storm put his head to one side as he looked up at her. "I am sorry that you are feeling sad, Lauren."

Lauren patted one of his soft little paws. "Thanks, Storm. You're sweet. But I'll just have to get over it, won't I? I'll be okay," she said softly.

Despite her good intentions about not getting into a bad mood, Lauren sat quietly staring out the car window the entire ride home.

Her mom frowned. "Are you feeling all right, honey? You don't have a stomachache or a headache, do you?"

"No. I'm okay," Lauren murmured.

"What's that you've got there in that drawstring bag?"

"Jemila's old skates. She said I can keep them, even though there's no chance of me using them now, is there?" Lauren said, looking at her mom hopefully.

Her mom gave her a sideways look. "I hope you're not going to ask about having figure-skating lessons again. Because I'm afraid you already know what the answer will be, don't you?" she said gently.

Lauren sighed and nodded.

The second she got inside the house, Lauren went into the kitchen to get herself a drink and grab two bags of potato chips before heading straight upstairs to be by herself with Storm. He seemed to be the only one who understood her, and she was really glad that she had him for a friend.

Her mom looked surprised as Lauren dashed past. "Where are you off to in such a hurry?"

"Got to . . . um, finish some homework!" Lauren called over her shoulder.

"I'll call you when supper's ready."

In her bedroom, Lauren put her bag down and Storm jumped out. They sat on her bedroom rug together and Lauren shared her chips with the tiny puppy.

Storm crunched them all up and then sat licking his chops. "Are you ready now?" he woofed, his big dewy eyes sparkling.

Lauren blinked at him in puzzlement. "Ready for what?"

Storm didn't answer. Lauren felt a warm tingling sensation flow down her spine as big gold sparks ignited in Storm's fluffy black fur and his little pointed ears fizzled and crackled with miniature lightning flashes.

Excitement glowed through Lauren. It felt like something very strange was about to happen.

Chapter
FIVE

Storm held up one tiny black front paw, and a big spurt of glittering sparkles shot into the air. Lauren watched in utter astonishment as the cloud of tiny sparks whizzed around faster and faster, until they became like an ice storm inside a Christmas snow globe.

The air in front of her shifted like a shimmering curtain, and the room began to change right in front of Lauren's very eyes.

Creak! The walls moved outward and the room stretched to six times its normal size. *Phut!* The bed, dresser, and other furniture shrank and lined itself up against one wall. *Crackle!* A small ice rink, with a rail around it, appeared in the center of the room.

There was a soft thud, and a book appeared on the ground beside her.

Lauren bent down to pick it up. The title read *Figure-Skating Techniques—Step by Step*.

"Wow! This is amazing!" Lauren exclaimed. She beamed at Storm. Now she knew what he'd been doing in the school library. "You've thought of everything. Now I can have a practice session. And this book is nearly as good as having a real coach all to myself!"

"I am glad that you are pleased," Storm woofed with a toothy little grin.

Lauren couldn't wait to try out the rink. She quickly changed out of her school clothes and put on Jemila's old skates.

"Here I go!" she said delightedly. She took a deep breath and glided onto the ice. It felt amazing to soar along so smoothly that it was almost as if she were flying. Her heart lifted as she knew for certain that this was all she wanted to do from now on.

After five minutes of skating, Lauren had warmed up and was ready to start work. She picked a simple routine from the book. After a few mistakes, she knew it by heart and started practicing to make it perfect.

As Lauren became more confident, she felt so happy. It was as if her feet had wings. "I can't believe how well I'm doing. You're not using your magic to make me skate better, are you?" she asked suspiciously, zooming past him with her arms outspread.

Storm was sitting at the edge of the rink watching her. He shook his head. "No, Lauren. I would not do that. It is better for you to learn by yourself. After all, I will not always be here to help you."

"It must be beginner's luck then . . ." Lauren stopped as Storm's words sank in. She skidded to a halt in a silvery spurt of ice crystals. "But Shadow won't find you here, will he? So you can live here with me always!"

Storm shook his head slowly, and his
tiny square face wore a serious expression.
"Shadow will never give up looking for
me. And I must one day return to my
home world to lead the Moon-claw
pack," he reminded her.

Lauren felt a pang. She didn't want
to think about her wonderful little friend
leaving when she'd barely gotten used to
having him around. "But that won't be for
a long time, will it?" she asked anxiously.

Storm's little black muzzle wrinkled
in a smile. "I will stay here for as long as I
can," he woofed.

"Yay! That's okay then! Watch this!"
Flexing her knees, Lauren shot across
the ice and did a rather squiggly figure
eight.

"That is very good, Lauren," Storm

yapped. "Perhaps I will try ice skating!"
There was another flash of sparks, and
tiny gold skates appeared on all four of his
little black paws. Storm zoomed forward
and glided across the ice in a straight line.
But the moment he lifted one front paw,
all the others shot out.

"Wur-rooof!" Storm collapsed onto
his tummy in a furry heap.

"Oh dear! Are you all right, Storm?"
Lauren skated over and picked up the

tiny puppy and set him firmly back on his paws. Her lips twitched, but she bit back a grin—she didn't want to hurt her friend's feelings.

Storm shook himself, flicking powdery ice crystals from his thick black fur. "It is a lot more difficult than it looks! I think that I will leave figure skating to you," he woofed, padding gingerly off the ice. As soon as he stepped onto the bedroom carpet, his tiny skates dissolved in a cloud of gold glitter.

An hour later Lauren was hot and sweaty and her legs were aching pleasantly. She glided up to the rail and stepped off the ice. Sitting down next to Storm, she started to remove her skates. "Phew! That was fantastic. Even Becky hasn't got her very own private skating rink! Thanks,

Storm—you are the best puppy ever!"

"You are welcome. Now you can practice every night after school," Storm woofed happily.

Lauren's eyes widened. "Really? I thought this was a special one-time treat! That's *so* amazing. I'm going to work hard and get really good. If I can prove to Mom and Dad that I'm serious about being a figure skater they'll *have* to let me join the Ice Academy!"

"Lauren! Dinner's ready!" her mom called upstairs a few minutes later.

"Coming!" Lauren sang out.

Storm raised his tiny black front paw again and Lauren felt a tingling down her spine as busy magical sparks changed her bedroom back to normal.

Happiness filled Lauren as she and

Storm went downstairs together. Storm was the best friend anyone could have.

"How did it go last night?" Lauren asked Jemila in class the following day. "Did Padmini, Katie, and Becky all sign up for figure-skating classes?"

"Yeah. They all joined. Maggie was really happy to have some new members. Becky turned up in a brand-new purple leotard and matching skates," Jemila told her.

Lauren laughed. "Of course she did!"

Jemila laughed, too. "She didn't look too impressed when she saw the uniforms we all have to wear—short pleated skirts and T-shirts aren't her style! She said they were like some boring old gym clothes!

Anyway, it was pretty fun. But I really wish
you could have been there."

"Me too," Lauren agreed. She wished
that she could tell Jemila about having
her own private magic ice rink, but she
knew that she could never give away
Storm's secret—not even to her best friend.

Lauren darted a secretive glance at
Storm, who was invisibly stretched out full-
length on her desk. He opened one sleepy

midnight-blue eye and his tail twitched.

"You *are* still coming to the normal Saturday morning sessions at the rink, aren't you?" Jemila asked.

Lauren nodded. "Yes. Mom and Dad are fine about me going to those. And I get my allowance on Saturdays, anyway."

"Great. We'll all be there as well," Jemila said. "We're starting to have classes on Saturdays, too. A part of the rink's going to be roped off for the academy."

"Is that because of the show in two weeks?" Lauren asked.

"Yes, but Maggie wants us all to work extra hard for the next few weeks. She said the best skaters will be offered a place at summer school."

"Wow!" Lauren was seriously impressed. Getting a place at figure-

skating summer school was beyond even
her wildest dreams. She had a thought.
"So you, Becky, Katie, and Padmini are
all going to be busy behind the roped-off
area on Saturday?" She sighed. It looked
like she was going to have to skate around
all by herself in the public area with lots of
kids she didn't know, which wouldn't be
nearly as much fun.

"Yeah, but if we all get there early, we
can have a normal skate together before
class starts in the academy section," Jemila
said. "I can show you some of the new
moves we've been doing, if you like."

"I'd love that!" Lauren enthused. *And
then with Storm's help I'll be able to practice
them in my bedroom every night after school,*
she thought.

Chapter
SIX

Lauren usually enjoyed school, but over the next few days she couldn't wait to get home. The second she got back, she shot straight upstairs and spent every spare moment before supper, and an hour or two before bed, too, skating on the rink in her magically transformed bedroom.

"I think I'd better have a quiet word with your class teacher," Lauren's dad decided on Friday evening, when Lauren and Storm came downstairs to get a drink in between figure-skating practice.

Taken by surprise, Lauren blinked at him. "Why?"

"You've been spending hours upstairs on your homework this past week. Your mom and I have hardly seen you. We're worried that you're having problems with your schoolwork," he said, looking concerned.

"No! I . . . um, haven't! Everything's fine . . . ," Lauren burbled, trying to think of an explanation. It would be really embarrassing if her dad went to the school and made a fuss. How was she going to get out of this? She threw a desperate glance at Storm.

Storm pricked his ears, and tiny gold

sparks flicked out of the ends. Lauren heard a *thud* behind her and turned to see that the library book was on the floor.

She quickly bent down to pick it up. "Oops, I . . . um, left it on the chair. I must have just knocked it off!"

Her dad frowned in surprise as he reached out and took the book from her. "What's this? *Figure-Skating Techniques*?" he read.

"It's for my . . . um . . . new school project on figure skating," Lauren fibbed. "I want it to be the best project I've ever done. That's why I've been spending lots of time on it. But I didn't tell you about it because . . ." —she had a flash of inspiration—". . . because I thought you'd just think I was trying to get you to let me take figure-skating classes," she finished in a rush.

"Ah, I see." Her dad gave her a searching look. "You're sure this isn't some new version of 'pester power'?"

"Definitely not!" Lauren said indignantly. "But I *am* still crazy about figure skating, like I said I would be."

Her dad raised his eyebrows. "Hmm. It's still early. As I remember it, BMX biking lasted a little while before you completely lost interest."

Lauren pulled a wry face. She couldn't deny that. "This is different, Dad. Just you wait and see!"

"I'll do that," her dad said, grinning. "I'd be happy to be proved wrong." He gave her arm a friendly squeeze before he went out into the yard to cut the grass.

Lauren's shoulders sagged with relief. "Phew! Thank goodness Dad fell for it. I just hope he doesn't ask me to show him my figure-skating project!"

Storm's bright eyes lit up. "It is no problem if he does!"

There was another small spurt of golden sparkles, and Lauren found herself holding a folder. She opened it. It was stuffed full of printed pages and pictures of ice-skaters.

"Just in case you need it," Storm yapped.

She gaped at the folder in amazement. "Where did all this work come from?"

Storm gave her a doggy grin. "There was a machine in the school library. It had lots of colored pictures on it. I sat and watched someone using it and saw how they got words and pictures to come out onto paper."

"You used your magic on a computer? Cool!" Lauren raised her eyebrows and smiled at Storm. He was certainly full of surprises. What else could he do?

Lauren was really excited on Saturday morning when her mom dropped her and Storm off at the White Water ice rink.

Lauren shouldered her red gym bag, with Storm inside it, as she went toward the girls' locker room.

She couldn't wait to see Jemila and her other school friends and show them how much her skating had improved.

"It's probably best if you watch from the rink-side seats. It can get crowded on the ice, and you might get hurt," Lauren whispered to Storm as she tied her skates.

Storm nodded and scampered off to find an empty chair.

Lauren came out of the locker room and made her way toward the ice.

"Hi, Lauren!" Jemila called as Lauren glided onto the ice. She was with Padmini, Katie, and Becky. They were all wearing their short pleated skirts and matching T-shirts, with Ice Academy in white letters.

Lauren skated over to join her friends.
She felt a bit odd in her ordinary jeans and
plain top. Becky might not have liked the
uniform, but Lauren would've loved to be
wearing it. "Hi, everyone!" she said brightly.

"Hi, Lauren!"

The girls linked arms and skated around
the rink together for a while. Then Becky,

Padmini, and Katie showed Lauren a new routine they were learning. Lauren began joining in, pleased to be included for once.

"You're really good, Lauren," Becky said. "Anyone would think you've been practicing as much as we have!"

Lauren grinned to herself. She stood by with her friends as Jemila demonstrated a more complicated move from the show. She watched closely, admiring the graceful swirls and sweeping movements. Jemila finished by doing an impressive spin and came to a stop with both arms raised in the air.

"Wow! That was fantastic!" Lauren exclaimed. "Watch me! I've learned some new moves. I might try and do a spin, too!"

"Wait! Be careful . . . ," Jemila warned.

But Lauren wasn't listening. She zoomed across the ice to get up speed. All her hours spent skating on her secret magical rink over the past week had given her confidence, and she felt as if she could do anything.

As Lauren came out of a long curve, she leaned forward and balanced on one leg while raising the other one behind her. Jemila and the other girls cheered. Lauren was enjoying herself so much that she got totally carried away. She took a deep breath and began to go into a twirl.

Lauren spun around faster and faster. Suddenly one skate seemed to slip out from under her. She went over on one ankle, lost her balance, and went sprawling backward.

"Oh!" she gasped as she sat down hard on her bottom.

Jemila rushed over to help Lauren get to her feet. "Are you okay? I tried to warn you about doing spins. It takes a lot of practice to get them right."

Lauren dusted powdery ice from her jeans, her face flushed. "I'm fine."

Padmini and Becky were both looking sympathetic.

Katie let out a shout of laughter. "Sorry, Lauren, but you looked so funny. You went down like a sack of potatoes!"

A group of older girls who were standing nearby nudged each other and laughed, too. "Yeah, she did!" one of them mocked.

Lauren ignored them. "Thanks a lot, Katie," she murmured, still feeling a bit shaken up.

She felt really silly for showing off in front of her friends, especially since the older girls had been watching, too. Lauren realized that she still had a long way to go before she was even half as good as Jemila. Having her own secret ice rink was fantastic, but it would never

be a substitute for belonging to the Ice
Academy.

A slim woman with a ponytail came
onto the ice. She waved and blew a
whistle.

"There's Maggie, our coach. It's time
for our class. We have to go over into the
roped-off area now. Why don't you come
and watch us, Lauren?" Padmini suggested.

"You might pick up a few tips," Becky
said.

"I think I need to," Lauren agreed in
a subdued voice. "I'm just going to get
changed first. I won't be long." As she came
off the ice and hobbled toward the changing
rooms she saw Storm jump down from his
chair beside the rink.

He pricked up his little black ears as
he came scampering toward her. "I saw you

fall. Have you hurt yourself?"

Lauren shook her head. "No. Just my pride. I'm fine now," she replied. There was no one else in the locker room as she sat on a bench to take off her skates. Lauren's red gym bag lay open next to her. Storm leaped straight inside in a *whoosh* of sparks and curled up.

"Hey! What are you doing with *my* gym bag?" called an annoyed voice.

Lauren looked up to see a girl who looked about thirteen years old coming toward her. It was the ringleader of the older girls who had laughed when she'd fallen over on the ice. She looked tough and unfriendly.

"It's not your bag. It's mine," Lauren said nervously.

"Yeah, right!" The older girl marched up to the bench, held up her hand, and prepared to drop her heavy skates into Lauren's bag—right on top of Storm!

Chapter
SEVEN

There was no time to think. Lauren moved like lightning. She grabbed her bag and pulled it toward her, at the same time thrusting out her free arm.

"Ow!" Pain crashed through Lauren as the skates swung against her elbow before clattering noisily to the floor. But she tried to ignore it as she made sure that

Storm hadn't been hurt.

Luckily the tiny puppy had jumped out of the bag when Lauren had grabbed it, and was now standing on the wooden bench. It had happened so fast that Storm looked stunned.

The older girl's eyes glinted with anger as she bent down to pick up her skates. "Hey! There's no need to take it out on

me, just because you're a pathetic
wannabe!"

"I didn't . . . I wasn't . . . ," Lauren
stammered. "Your skates would have
hurt St—" She stopped as she realized
that there was no way she could explain
about her invisible magical friend. She
was struggling to find something to say
when she caught a flash of something red
out of the corner of her eye. An identical
gym bag was hanging from a nearby coat
hook.

"Look! That's your red bag!" Lauren
said, pointing.

The older girl looked at the bag and
her face changed. "Oh . . . right. Sorry!
Gotta go!" She grabbed the red bag,
stuffed her skates inside, and hurried away.

Lauren crumpled. Now that the

danger to Storm was over she felt
all wobbly, and her injured arm was
throbbing like crazy. She was glad that no
one else had seen what had happened,
and now that the other girl had gone, the
locker room was empty again.

Storm seemed to have recovered.
"Thank you for saving me," he woofed
and then his bright blue eyes clouded.
"But you are hurt. I will make you
better."

Lauren felt a familiar warm prickling
sensation down her spine as Storm
leaned forward and huffed out a warm
puppy breath that glowed with thousands
of tiny glittering gold stars. The
shimmering mist surrounded Lauren's
arm, and she felt a soothing sensation—
just as if cool fingers were massaging the

pain away. It seemed to run down her arm and flow out of the ends of her fingers.

"It's much better now. Thanks, Storm."

Storm jumped onto the floor. "Shall we go and watch Jemila and the other girls now?"

Lauren nodded. But as she and Storm went back toward the rink, she was still smarting with humiliation at having made a fool of herself. She seemed to hear the older girl's words ringing in her head:

You're a pathetic wannabe.

Maybe I am, Lauren thought glumly. *Maybe all I'll ever be is a wannabe.*

Sunday dawned bright and clear. Lauren and Storm went to a flea market with her mom and dad in the afternoon.

She was feeling a bit better today, having decided to put what had happened in the locker room yesterday behind her. But she couldn't completely forget what the older girl had said.

The park was bustling with people wandering around tables full of interesting things. Larger items like furniture, kids' bikes, and playpens stood on the grass.

Storm ran around invisibly, enjoying all the interesting smells. Lauren could see his furry little black shape dodging between the people wandering around.

When Lauren stopped to look at a stall selling pretty barrettes, Storm dived beneath the table and began nosing through a box of toys. Moments later he emerged with a hideous bright-pink

plastic rabbit held proudly in his mouth.

Lauren almost fell down laughing
as Storm chomped on the toy with his
sharp puppy teeth.

Squeak! Squeak!

Luckily, with all the noise and activity,
no one had noticed that the squeaky toy
appeared to be floating in midair. Lauren
quickly bent down and held out her hand.

"Storm! Give it here!" she whispered.

Storm shook his head, his midnight-blue eyes gleaming mischievously. He wagged his stumpy black tail and bounced down onto his front paws.

"I know you want to play, but you'll have to wait until we get home. There are too many people around here," Lauren said, trying to sound firm. "Now, give me that rabbit, please. I'll buy it for you."

Storm opened his mouth reluctantly and the toy dropped to the grass. Lauren picked it up and paid for it. As she wandered off with Storm at her heels to look at something else, she saw Katie walking toward her.

"Hi!" she called, waving the arm holding Storm's toy.

"What is *that*?" Katie said, laughing,

pointing at the bright-pink plastic
toy. "Have you got a new pet dog or
something?"

Lauren grinned. "As if! I just . . . um,
love collecting really horrible, cheapo toys.
Is Becky with you?" she asked, quickly
changing the subject before she had to
answer any more awkward questions.

"Becky wouldn't be seen dead at
a flea market!" Katie said. "She's asked
Jemila and Padmini to go and see *The Ice
Princess* with her. I couldn't go because I
was already going out with my mom, but
I thought Becky said she was going to call
you to ask if you wanted to go, too."

Lauren would have loved to have
gone to see the movie. She couldn't
help wondering whether Becky hadn't
bothered to call her, now that Lauren

wasn't part of the new figure-skating gang.

Katie saw the look on Lauren's face. "You'd probably already left with your mom and dad by the time Becky called," she guessed.

Lauren cheered up a bit. That could be true. Becky might be careless sometimes, but she wasn't mean.

"Do you feel like getting a burger?" Katie asked.

At the mention of food, Storm barked eagerly. He jumped up and pawed at Lauren's leg. "I like human food!" he panted.

Lauren grinned at the tiny puppy's bright little face and then turned to Katie. "Why not? The others don't know what they're missing!"

They bought burgers and wandered

around eating them. Lauren made sure
that Katie didn't notice her breaking off
tiny pieces and dropping them onto the
grass for Storm to gobble up.

After Katie said good-bye and went off
with her mom, Lauren and Storm slowly
made their way back toward her parents'
car, where she'd arranged to meet up with
her mom and dad.

Suddenly Storm gave a yelp of terror and streaked toward some nearby bushes.

"Storm?" Lauren frowned as she went to find her little puppy friend.

She reached the bushes and bent down to peer into the branches. She could see Storm crouched into a tight ball. His ears were laid back and he was trembling all over.

"What's wrong? Are you sick?" she asked worriedly.

"Shadow has found me. He has put a spell on those dogs!" Storm whimpered, his midnight-blue eyes wide and fearful.

"What dogs, Storm?" Lauren looked up to see a nearby woman with two large dogs on leashes. One of them was barking excitely. The woman opened her car, and the dogs jumped inside the backseat.

"I don't *think* those dogs are after you. But how can I tell if they're under a magic spell?" Lauren asked.

Storm burrowed deeper into the bushes. "They will have fierce pale eyes and extra-large teeth. And be very fierce and strong."

Lauren looked hard at the dogs in the back of the car as the woman drove slowly past her on the way to the exit. "Those dogs don't look like that. I think they're normal. Anyway, they're gone now. You can come out."

Lauren picked Storm up as he crawled out from the bush on wobbly little legs. "Poor you. You've had a big scare," she whispered, stroking him gently. "Let's get into our car. Here's Mom and Dad now. We'll be home soon."

As Lauren sat in the back of the car
with Storm on her lap, she felt his little
heart fluttering against her hand. The
glimpse of possible danger made her
realize all over again that Storm might
have to leave suddenly in order to save
himself.

Lauren felt a pang as she thought that however much she might try to prepare herself for losing Storm, she would never be ready to let him go.

Chapter
EIGHT

A few days later, Lauren was skating around the magical ice rink in her bedroom, after she had helped clean up after supper. Storm sat watching her. He was completely recovered from his scare at the flea market, and there had been no sign of any of Shadow's dogs.

"Phew!" Lauren panted as she zoomed toward the rail and leaned on it to catch her breath. She felt hot and sticky after practicing for an hour and a half. "I just can't get my head around this new routine. I'm starting to think that I'll never be any good at this."

Storm wagged his tail encouragingly. "You are making very good progress, Lauren!"

"Do you really think so?" Lauren smiled at her loyal little friend.

It was really hard to keep practicing in secret without any of her friends to give her encouragement. And, although she had tried to put it behind her, her self-confidence had been shaken by what had happened at the White Water ice rink.

Lauren's damp hair was sticking to her hot face. She wiped it on a towel. "Maybe I'm just kidding myself. I'll never be good enough to be a figure skater, and Mom and Dad will never let me join the Ice Academy," she said dejectedly.

Storm's furry black brow wrinkled in a frown. "But you are getting better all the time. I know how much you love figure skating, and you are working very hard at it. You just have to believe in yourself,

Lauren," he yapped.

"I know you're right. But that's the hardest part." Lauren sighed. She was beginning to wonder if she really could do it all by herself—even with Storm's help.

She came off the ice and sat down on her rug to unlace her skates. Storm raised a tiny front paw, and glitter swirled around as the ice rink disappeared and her bedroom shrank and went back to normal.

Lauren slowly got to her feet. Her leg muscles were aching and she felt tired all over.

She could hear the TV on in the living room, where her dad sat watching a wildlife documentary. Her mom had gone out to the golf course with a couple of her friends from work. It was dark outside, and Lauren closed the curtains.

When she turned back to the bedroom, Storm was sitting on her bed beside her open figure-skating book. He was resting one tiny front paw on a page and looking closely at a brightly colored picture.

Lauren bent over to see what he was so interested in. "That's Naomi Teal in *The Sleeping Beauty on Ice*. She's my favorite skater. I'd love to be just like her." She sighed sadly, thinking that she could never be that good. "I'm going down to say good night to Dad and then I'm going to bed. Do you want me to let you out into the backyard for a quick run first?"

Storm nodded and followed her out.

Lauren put on her pajamas and then jumped into bed. She was just settling down with Storm cuddled up in the crook of her arm when she felt a familiar warm prickling sensation down her spine.

"Storm? What are you up to?" she yawned.

Storm's midnight-blue eyes glowed like jewels as his fluffy black fur ignited with dazzling gold sparks and his ears and tail crackled with electricity.

The bed began to shake, and a golden glow appeared around her. Lauren's eyes shot open and she sat upright, suddenly wide awake.

Woo-oosh! Shimmering pillars of light stretched upward around her and joined together to form ornate walls and a door of golden metal and glass. *Rustle!* Lauren found herself wrapped in feather-soft blankets and sitting on soft cushions inside a fabulous coach. *Jingle!* A team of magnificent white horses was harnessed to the front.

The next instant the horses leaped upward in a multicolored spray of sparks. The golden coach zoomed straight *through* the ceiling and sped across the night sky, which was pricked by millions of bright stars.

Lauren was transfixed with wonder. "Where are we going?" she gasped.

"Wait and see!" Storm woofed mysteriously. He sat in her lap and she held his warm little body close as they streaked onward. It seemed like no time at all before the horses' hooves were skimming across snow-covered treetops, and then the coach was speeding downward toward a frozen lake.

"Wow! There's a show on!" Lauren gasped as she saw the brightly colored

lights and the figure skaters' beautiful
sparkling costumes. An ice castle with
turrets and towers, which was lit from
within with candles, glowed like a giant,
flickering jewel.

A big crowd of people was watching
the skaters, while others were strolling
around stalls that were set out around the
lake's edges. The golden coach landed on
a deserted strip of narrow land on the
far shore. No one paid any attention and
Lauren realized that they must be invisible.

She had a great view from here and
leaned forward from inside the warm
coach to watch the skaters as they swirled
and skimmed across the ice.

"This is like something from a fairy
tale. Those skaters are amazing!" Lauren
enthused. Her breath fogged in the frosty

air, but Storm's magic stopped her from feeling the slightest bit cold. Suddenly Lauren spotted a face she recognized. "I can't believe it! That's Naomi Teal!"

"I know," Storm woofed, looking very pleased with himself.

Lauren watched the show for the next hour and a half, lost in the wonder of the whole spectacle. This was the best night of her life! As the glittering performance came to an end, the skaters took their bows and the audience's cheers rang out across the lake.

There was a golden flash and the coach and horses rose into the air in another swirling snowstorm of sparks as the horses drew them homeward. With a final fizzle of light and a loud *pop!* the coach and horses dissolved, and Lauren found herself back in bed.

"That was so amazing. Thanks, Storm! I'll never forget this night!"

Storm's little black muzzle wrinkled in a smile. "You are welcome."

"I wish I could skate like that," Lauren murmured, stifling a yawn.

Storm looked up at her and placed one tiny front paw on her cheek. "You will one day, Lauren."

"Do you really think so?" Lauren asked, looking down into his little face.

Storm nodded. "Yes, I do. But you will have to be very determined and hold on to your dreams. And you must not let setbacks get you down."

Just like you, Lauren thought, feeling proud of her brave little friend who was determined one day to lead the Moon-

claw pack, despite the danger from
Shadow.

Her heart seemed to swell with new
purpose.

"You're right, Storm. From now on,
I'm going to work *extra* hard. I'll practice
on my magical rink every moment I can,
and nothing is going to make me stop!"
If Storm believed in her, she could do it!
She stroked the top of the tiny puppy's
soft little head. "What would I do without
you?" she whispered sleepily as she
snuggled under the covers.

Chapter
NINE

Lauren kept her promise to herself, and over the following ten days she threw herself into ice-skating practice with renewed enthusiasm. The time seemed to fly by and then it was the day before the show.

"It's the final dress rehearsal tonight," Jemila told Lauren nervously after school. "You wouldn't come with me, would you?"

"Me?" Lauren said, surprised. "What about Katie, Becky, and Padmini, won't they be there?"

Jemila wrinkled her nose. "Yeah, but it's not the same. You're my best friend."

Lauren smiled. "Of course I'll come! I'd love to."

"Great." Jemila beamed at her. "I'll meet you outside the rink. It's closed, except for skaters or people working on the show, but I know Maggie won't mind. She said we always need extra helpers.

Besides, I've told her all about how you would love to be a figure skater."

"Have you?" Lauren said, amazed that Jemila had spoken to the figure-skating coach about her. "What did she say?"

"Maggie thought it was a shame that your parents wouldn't let you join the Ice Academy when you were so excited about it. Anyway, bring your skates. You should be able to grab some free time on the ice when we have a break in rehearsals."

"Okay. Sounds great." Lauren smiled, feeling excited already. "See you there."

"Well, I have to say that you do seem to be sticking with figure skating," Lauren's dad commented as she and Storm got out of the car in front of the rink later that evening. "Maybe the third time's the charm."

"It is!" Lauren exclaimed. She waved to Jemila, who was waiting for her at the ice-rink entrance. She bent down to smile in through the passenger window at her dad. "So does that mean you'll let me join the Ice Academy?" she asked playfully.

"Hmm. We'll see," he said, smiling. "See you later."

"Did you hear that?" Lauren whispered to Storm excitedly as her dad drove away. "I really think I might be allowed to join the academy soon!"

Storm was sitting with his paws looped over her gym bag. He twisted his head around to look up at her. "That is good!"

Lauren ruffled the soft fur on his little head. "Thank you for making me realize that my dream about being an ice-skater could come true if I didn't give up. I know now that I'm never, ever going to stop!" she said.

Storm wagged his stumpy black tail.

Lauren and Storm went inside the rink with Jemila. The whole place was transformed. The rink was strung with

Christmas lights, plastic icicles, and flowing white ribbons. Painted cardboard scenery made it into a magical winter forest, with snowy hills and a white castle glistening in the distance.

"Wow! Look at this!" Lauren said. It made her think of her wonderful night journey across the starry sky to the show on the frozen lake.

But Jemila seemed too nervous to reply. Lauren went into the changing rooms with her. Becky, Padmini, and Katie were already there and changing into their costumes. They were going to do a simple routine dressed as forest animals.

As Lauren was helping Jemila into her glittering white costume and matching skates, Maggie came in. The coach had her hair tied back in a ponytail.

Maggie greeted all the girls and gave Lauren a friendly smile before ushering everyone outside to begin the rehearsal.

For the next hour, Lauren helped out where she could and then kept out of the way while Maggie put the skaters through their paces. Lauren felt her feet twitching to join in as she watched the girls skating around the ice. She clapped enthusiastically as they performed routine after routine.

"One day, huh?" she whispered to Storm, who sat beside her.

Storm nodded vigorously, his tail twirling.

"Take twenty, everyone!" Maggie called. She led the way off the ice and all the young skaters went to get drinks and relax for a while.

Jemila came over to Lauren. "Why don't you find a quiet bit of the rink and skate a little? No one will mind."

"Okay." Lauren didn't need to be told twice.

She quickly put on her skates and glided onto the ice. As music flooded out over the sound system, Lauren lost herself and skated for pure joy. She was so engrossed in the figure-skating routine, which she'd learned by heart, that she didn't notice the little puff of gold sparkles that fizzed into the air above where Storm was sitting watching. A spotlight

began following Lauren across the ice.

Lauren skated on in a world of her own. As she finally swept to a graceful halt she heard clapping.

"Bravo!" called a voice.

Startled, Lauren whipped around to see Maggie walking across the ice toward her. She felt herself turning bright red.

"Well done, Lauren! Jemila told me you were good, but I wanted to see for myself," Maggie said. "And there you were, caught in the spotlight, so I couldn't help but notice you. How lucky was that? How would you like to come to our summer skating school?"

"Really? I'd love to!" Lauren burst out delightedly. "But how can I? I don't belong to the Ice Academy."

Maggie smiled warmly. "We'll see

about that. You leave it to me."

Lauren left the ice in a daze. She couldn't wait to tell Storm her wonderful news. But as she walked toward him he jumped down and shot toward a storeroom.

Lauren headed for a large piece of scenery that was propped beside the open storeroom doorway, almost blocking off the inside. Suddenly she heard a fierce growling. Dark shapes were prowling along the corridor, coming closer. The lights gleamed on their cold pale eyes and their extra-long teeth.

Lauren's blood ran cold. Shadow's dogs! Storm was in terrible danger.

She dashed around the scenery and squeezed into the storeroom, just as there was a dazzling flash of bright golden light, which lit up the entire room. Storm stood there, a tiny, helpless puppy no longer, but his true majestic self: a handsome young silver-gray wolf with a sparkling neck ruff and glowing midnight-blue eyes. An older wolf with a gentle face, who Lauren guessed was his mother, stood next to him.

And then Lauren knew that Storm was

leaving for good. She was going to have to be very brave. She rushed over and the huge wolf allowed her to hug him one last time.

"I'll never forget you, Storm," Lauren said, her voice breaking as she buried her face in his thick, soft fur.

"You have been a very good friend, Lauren. I will always remember you," Storm said in a deep, velvety growl.

Lauren took a step back just as an ugly snarl sounded right outside, beside the scenery. "Go. Save yourself, Storm!" she urged in a choked voice.

There was a final flash of light and a silent explosion of bright gold sparks that drifted down around Lauren and fizzled out harmlessly on the storeroom floor. Storm and his mother faded and then were gone. The growl was abruptly cut off and silence fell.

Lauren stood there, her heart aching with sadness. She was going to miss Storm terribly, but at least she knew he was safe. And she would always have her secret memories of the wonderful adventure they'd shared.

"Lauren? Where are you?" called Jemila's voice from the corridor. "Your dad's looking for you. Maggie's just been talking to him, and he's got a huge smile on his face!"

"Coming!" Lauren called. She brushed away a tear as she went out with new hope in her heart. "Thanks, Storm, for helping to make my dreams come true! I really hope yours come true, too," she whispered.

About the Author

Sue Bentley's books for children often
include animals, fairies, and wildlife. She
lives in Northampton, England, and enjoys
reading, going to the movies, relaxing
by her garden pond, and watching the
birds feeding their babies on the lawn.
At school she was always getting told off
for daydreaming or staring out of the
window—but she now realizes that she
was storing up ideas for when she became
a writer. She has met and owned many
cats and dogs, and each one has brought a
special kind of magic to her life.

Don't miss these Magic Ponies books!

Don't miss these Magic Kitten books!

Don't miss these
Magic Puppy books!

Don't miss these Magic Bunny books!